6119

WONDER BOOKS®

The
Revolutionary War

A Level Three Reader

By Cynthia Klingel and Robert B. Noyed

The **Child's World®**

On the cover...
This painting shows the Battle of Bunker Hill.

Published by The Child's World®, Inc.
PO Box 326
Chanhassen, MN 55317-0326
800-599-READ
www.childsworld.com

Photo Credits
© Bettmann/CORBIS: 17
© CORBIS: 13, 26
© David Muench/CORBIS: 25
© Hulton Archives: 14
© Jeff Greenberg/Unicorn Stock Photos: cover
© North Wind Pictures: 5, 18
© Photri, Inc.: 6, 10, 21, 22
© 2002 Stock Montage: 9, 29

Project Coordination: Editorial Directions, Inc.
Photo Research: Alice K. Flanagan

Library of Congress Cataloging-in-Publication Data
Klingel, Cynthia Fitterer.
The Revolutionary War / by Cynthia Klingel and Robert B. Noyed.
    p. cm.
ISBN 1-56766-961-1 (alk. paper)
1. United States—History—Revolution, 1775-1783—Juvenile literature.
[1. United States—History—Revolution, 1775-1783.]   I.Noyed, Robert B. II. Title.
E208 .K6 2001
973.3—dc21
                                    00-013176

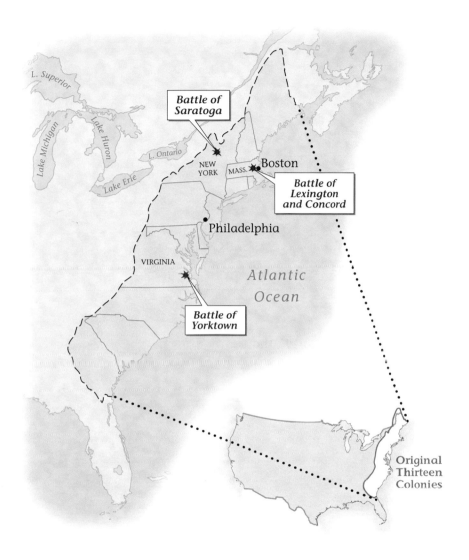

Do you know where the Revolutionary War took place? Here is a map to help you find out.

3

In the early 1770s, England ruled the American **colonies**. Many people in the colonies wanted their freedom. The people in the colonies were called **colonists.**

This is a drawing of colonists meeting →
a Native American named Squanto.

The king of England forced the colonists to pay taxes on many things. Many colonists did not like paying these taxes. One of the things that the king taxed was tea.

Here a drawing shows British ships carrying tea and other goods to the colonists.

In December of 1773, a group of colonists **rebelled** against the tea tax. They went onto English ships and threw the ships' tea into Boston Harbor. This was called the Boston Tea Party.

This illustration shows a group of colonists throwing tea into Boston Harbor. →

The Boston Tea Party made the king angry. He passed more laws to punish the colonists. He sent soldiers to control the colonists. The colonists grew angrier.

British soldiers wore uniforms like these during the Revolutionary War.

The colonists met secretly and formed an army. This **volunteer** army was called a **militia**. The colonists were ready to fight for their freedom.

This drawing shows an American militia volunteer.

13

To the King's Most Excellent Majesty.

Most Gracious Sovereign!

We your Majesty's faithful Subjects of the colonies of New-Hampshire, Massachusetts-Bay, Rhode-Island and Providence Plantations, Connecticut, New-York, New-Jersey, Pensylvania, the Counties of New-Castle, Kent and Sussex on Delaware, Maryland, Virginia, North-Carolina, and South-Carolina, in behalf of ourselves and the inhabitants of those colonies who have deputed us to represent them in General Congress, by this our humble petition, beg leave to lay our grievances before the throne.

A standing army has been kept in these colonies, ever since the conclusion of the late war, without the consent of our assemblies, and this army with a considerable naval armament has been employed to enforce the collection of taxes.

The Authority of the Commander in Chief, and, under him, of the Brigadiers General has in time of peace, been rendered supreme in all the civil governments in America.

The Commander in Chief of all your Majesty's forces in North-America has, in time of peace, been appointed Governor

Men from almost every colony formed a group called the Continental Congress. They met to find peaceful ways to solve their problems with the king. They were not successful. They then prepared for war with England.

Here you can see a letter from the colonists complaining to the king of England.

General George Washington led the American army. The first battle of the war was the Battle of Lexington and Concord. It took place in April of 1775. The English soldiers were called "redcoats" because they wore red coats.

This painting shows the Battle of Lexington and Concord. →

The battles continued. In 1776, the Continental Congress met again in Philadelphia, Pennsylvania. After many meetings, the Congress signed the Declaration of Independence on July 4, 1776.

This drawing shows men signing the Declaration of Independence.

Signing the declaration meant the colonists no longer wanted to be ruled by the king. They would continue to fight for their freedom. They knew it would not be easy.

This painting shows soldiers during the Revolutionary War.

The colonists were not trained to be soldiers. They also did not have enough supplies for the war. Many soldiers died during the war from sickness and from the cold weather.

This painting shows American soldiers during the winter. George Washington is on the white horse.

The war was hard for the colonists. Often they thought the English might win. But the colonists won the Battle of Saratoga in October of 1777. Now it was possible for the colonists to win the war.

This is what the battlefield at Saratoga looks like today. →

The last battle of the war was the Battle of Yorktown. The English army **surrendered** to the Americans on October 17, 1781. The Americans and the English signed a peace **treaty** in 1783.

This drawing shows the Battle of Yorktown.

The colonists had won their freedom from England. The king would no longer rule them. They were now ready to build their own free country. It would be called the United States of America.

Here you can see George Washington taking office as the first president of the United States. →

Glossary

colonies (KOL-uh-neez)
Colonies are lands ruled by a
faraway country.

colonists (KOL-uh-nists)
Colonists are people who live in
a colony.

militia (muh-LISH-uh)
A militia is a group of people
trained to fight in times of
emergencies.

rebelled (ree-BELD)
People who have rebelled have
fought against something.

surrendered (sur-REN-derd)
People who have surrendered
have given up a fight.

treaty (TREE-tee)
A treaty is a formal agreement
between countries.

volunteer (vol-un-TEER)
A volunteer does something
without getting paid.

Index

Battle of Lexington
    and Concord, 16
Battle of Saratoga, 24
Battle of Yorktown, 27
Boston Harbor, 8
Boston Tea Party, 8, 11
Continental Congress, 15, 19
Declaration of Independence,
    19, 20
freedom, 4, 12, 20, 28
king of England, 7, 11, 15,
    20, 28
militia, 12
Philadelphia, Pennsylvania, 19
"redcoats", 16
tea tax, 7, 8
treaty, 27
war, 15, 16, 23, 24, 27
Washington, George, 16

To Find Out More

Books

Giblin, James Cross. *George Washington: A Picture Book Biography.*
New York: Scholastic, 1998.

Osborne, Mary Pope. *Revolutionary War on Wednesday.* New York:
Random House Children's Publishing, 2000.

Roop, Peter, and Connie Roop. *Buttons for General Washington.*
Minneapolis, Minn.: Carolrhoda Books, 1986.

Web Sites

Liberty!: The American Revolution
http://www.pbs.org/ktca/liberty/
For facts about the Revolutionary War from the PBS documentary.

The National Park Service: Places of the Revolution
http://www.nps.gov/lhst/places.htm
For information on different Revolutionary War sites.

Spy Letters of the American Revolution
http://www.clements.umich.edu/spies/index-people.html
For lots of interesting information about Revolutionary War spies.

Note to Parents and Educators

Welcome to The Wonders of Reading™! These books provide text at three different levels for beginning readers to practice and strengthen their reading skills. In addition, the use of nonfiction text gives readers the valuable opportunity to *read to learn*, not just to learn to read.

These leveled readers allow children to choose books at their level of reading confidence and performance. Level One books offer beginning readers simple language, word choice, and sentence structure as well as a word list. Level Two books feature slightly more difficult vocabulary, longer sentences, and longer total text. In the back of each Level Two book are an index and a list of books and Web sites for finding out more information. Level Three books continue to extend word choice and length of text. In the back of each Level Three book are a glossary, an index, and a list of books and Web sites for further research.

State and national standards in reading and language arts emphasize using nonfiction at all levels of reading development. The Wonders of Reading™ books fill the historical void in nonfiction for primary grade readers with the additional benefit of a leveled text.

About the Authors

Cynthia Klingel has worked as a high school English teacher and an elementary teacher. She is currently the curriculum director for a Minnesota school district. Writing children's books is another way for her to continue her passion for sharing the written word with children. Cynthia is a frequent visitor to the children's section of bookstores and enjoys spending time with her many friends, family, and two daughters.

Robert Noyed started his career as a newspaper reporter. Since then, he has worked in communications and public relations for more than fourteen years for a Minnesota school district. He enjoys writing books for children and finds that it brings a different feeling of challenge and accomplishment from other writing projects. He is an avid reader who also enjoys music, theater, traveling, and spending time with his wife, son, and daughter.